For Pat and Ron

This paperback edition first published in Great Britain
in 2018 by Andersen Press Ltd.
First published in Great Britain in 2017 by
Andersen Press Ltd., 20 Vauxhall Bridge Road,
London SW1V 2SA.

1   3   5   7   9   10   8   6   4   2

British Library Cataloguing in Publication Data available.
ISBN 978 1 78344 592 9

REECE WYKES

I DARE YOU

Andersen Press

I'm bored.

I dare you...

to eat this bug!

Well, I dare you...

to eat this bird.

Right. I dare you...

to eat this rock.

to eat
this tree.

DONE. I dare you...

to eat ME!

you look bored.

This book belongs to: